THE FIREBIRD

THE FIREBIRD

AND OTHER
RUSSIAN FAIRY TALES

❖❖❖❖

Illustrations by Boris Zvorykin

Edited and with an Introduction by Jacqueline Onassis

A Studio Book

The Viking Press
New York

B. Z.

The Editor and the Publishers
wish to thank
Andreas Brown of the Gotham Book Mart
for bringing Boris Zvorykin's
original manuscript to their attention
and Gail Harrison
for her valuable research assistance

Introduction and English language translation
Copyright © Viking Penguin Inc., 1978
All rights reserved
First published in 1978 by The Viking Press
625 Madison Avenue, New York, N.Y. 10022
Published simultaneously in Canada by
Penguin Books Canada Limited

Library of Congress Cataloging in Publication Data
Main entry under title:
The Firebird and other Russian fairy tales.
(A Studio book)
Translation of Zhar-ptītsa, Vasilisa prekrasnaia, Mariia Morevna,
and Snegurochka. Originally translated by B. Zvorykin into French with title
L'Oiseau de feu et d'autres contes populaires russes, as a single
handpainted presentation volume in calligraphy. The original illustrations
are reproduced in this translation.
Summary: Retells four Russian folk tales: The Firebird, Vassilissa
the Fair, Maria Morevna, and The Snow Maiden.
1. Tales, Russian. [1. Folklore—Russia]
I. Zvorykin, Boris Vasil'evich, b. 1872.
II. Onassis, Jacqueline, 1929–
PZ8.1.F54   398.2'0947   78-5235
ISBN 0–670–31544–3

Printed in the United States of America

Set in Caslon

CONTENTS

INTRODUCTION

This book introduces, to readers old and young, a forgotten master of Russian decorative art, Boris Zvorykin, who was one of the last and most impressive artists in the great Russian tradition of book illustration. Zvorykin left Russia after the Revolution and settled finally in Paris, where he found employment in the publishing house of H. Piazza. There he made the original of this book, his own version of fairy stories as a present for his employer, Louis Fricotelle. He translated four Russian tales into French, writing them out in beautiful calligraphy and illustrating them on heavy vellum pages, which he then bound in red Moroccan leather embossed with Russian motifs. It was a gift of gratitude for a new life, celebrating all he valued and missed in the old.

Boris Vassilievich Zvorykin was born in Moscow in 1872, the son of merchant parents. After his graduation from the Moscow Academy of Painting, he decided to devote himself to decorative art, especially book decoration. He worked for several publishing houses, eventually joining the firm of A. A. Levenson, pioneers of *éditions de luxe* in Russia, and he remained there as art director for twenty years. He illustrated many books in the style of illuminated manuscripts and his reputation grew to rival that of Ivan Bilibin, the great illustrator of fairy tales whose books were always given as presentation copies to the Tsar's children even up to 1917.

Zvorykin painted the murals for the old Cathedral at Simferopol and received other important commissions from the Imperial Court, notably a book commemorating the tercentenary of the House of Romanov. He also illustrated a magnificent book about the Theodorovsky Cathedral at Tsarskoe Selo, which was published under the patronage of the Tsar.

Zvorykin's final great work before he left Russia was done to celebrate the re-establishment of the Patriarchal Throne in Russia, an illuminated rendition of the epistle of the Sacred Council confirming the election of the first Patriarch. This epistle was over twenty meters long and ornamented in the style of Russian seventeenth-century painting. He also designed the Patriarchal Seal for the church, and the personal epistles of the Patriarch.

Boris Zvorykin was a product of the Slavic Revival movement, which encouraged artists to travel throughout the land to search for the folk motifs of old Russia and incorporate them into contemporary art. In Moscow the movement was centered on the artists' colony at Abramtsevo, the country estate of a generous industrialist, Savva Mamontov. Konstantin Stanislavsky, founder of the Moscow Art Theatre, visited Abramtsevo regularly and noted that "Mamontov was in charge of all the activities and at the same time wrote plays, joked with the young people, dictated business letters and telegrams connected with his complicated railroad affairs."

Mamontov brought together artists from all fields at Abramtsevo and many of them, including Stanislavsky, worked on productions for his company, the Nikolai Krotkov Opera Troupe. The painter who first influenced Zvorykin, Elena Polenova, was a member of Abramtsevo, as was Viktor Vasnetsov, a painter of Russian historical scenes whose disciple Zvorykin later became.

In the capital, St. Petersburg, the artistic center was the World of Art group, a movement of artists and aesthetes led by Sergei Diaghilev and Alexandre Benois. Their intention was to redefine the tradition of Russian decorative arts in a reaction against the suffocating influence of the Imperial theaters and against audiences whom Diaghilev called "sickly sentimentalists fainting away to the sounds of Mendelssohn *lieder*."

Out of this group came one of the artistic wonders of the twentieth century, the Ballets Russes, which burst upon the West in 1909, when Diaghilev overwhelmed Paris with his production of the Polovtsian Dances from Borodin's *Prince Igor,* for which Nicholas Roerich had designed the sets.

Over the next five years Diaghilev followed this triumph with productions of *The Firebird, Scheherezade, Petrushka,* and *Le Coq d'Or* with sets by Alexander Golovin, Léon Bakst, Benois, and Natalia Goncharova and with scores by Stravinsky and Rimsky-Korsakov. The decor and the music as well as the stories on which these works were based reflected the same interest in Russian history and the same love of colorful rhythmic expression as that of the Abramtsevo group.

In fact, the two groups were closely connected in many ways. They worked on each other's productions, illustrated books for the same publishers, wrote for the same magazines, and went to Paris together with the Russian contribution to the *Salon d'Automne* exhibition and with the Ballets Russes. Although there is little documentation of the fact, Zvorykin must have known them all and worked among them. His selection of fairy tales for his gift to Fricotelle and his manner of illustrating them are strongly influenced by the intense interest the two groups showed in Russian tradition.

Two of the tales he selected, "The Firebird" and "The Snow Maiden," had been presented in the form of operas and ballet and are quintessentially Russian. In fact they could have originated in no other country. We see, hear, and smell Russia in their lines: the damp black earth, the dense forest, the snow in deep winter, the wooden huts or "isbas" of the peasants and their lively village dances.

In "The Snow Maiden" we see scenes of Russian feudal life: the local rulers' great wooden dwellings with iron grille doors and wooden floors and benches covered by Oriental carpets, settings where the Tsar and his nobles, his "boyars," feasted from golden goblets and plates, dressed in barbaric splendor in their fur hats and brocade kaftans embroidered with jewels.

Even the supernatural beings in these tales are uniquely Russian, from Baba Yaga, the gruesome witch, to the Firebird, symbol of life, embodiment of sun and fire, a radiant being opposed to the demon of evil, the snakelike Koshchey the Deathless, a personification of the dreaded Tatar. Dark and light, fire and cold, the extremes of climate and personality are Russian indeed.

The telling of tales was an old tradition in Russia. Tsars and Tsarinas had storytellers to while away the hours for them, and blind men used to apply for positions as tellers of tales in rich houses. The oral style of the folk tale was important to the development of Russia's great prose writers, Tolstoy, Pushkin and Dostoevsky among others, and its imagery enriched her poets. Tolstoy remembered bedtime stories told him by an old serf whom his grandfather had bought simply because he knew so many tales and told them so well. And these stories, too, should be told or read aloud, rather than silently absorbed. Only then can one really appreciate the rich drama and fantastic imagery of Russian fairy tales that have been related to generation after generation of mesmerized listeners of all ages.

Russian folk and fairy tales were first collected from every region of the country by the ethnographer Alexander Afanas'ev and published, together with a study of their symbolism, in many volumes beginning in 1866. No child's bookshelf was complete without his volumes, and the tales he published became part of the consciousness of every Russian from childhood on. Sergei Esenin, the Russian poet and first husband of Isadora Duncan, is said to have searched for Afanas'ev's books during the hungry years of the civil war (1918-1920) and paid for one copy with three bushels of wheat.

At some point in the 1920s, years after the Russia he knew had disappeared, Boris Zvorykin, in exile with many of his former colleagues, tried to recapture the richness of that distant culture he held in his heart. Against a background of gray Paris skies and mansard roofs, he painstakingly wrote out in French the Russian phrases long familiar to him, and brushed his brilliant colors into the pictures of onion domes and flowing rivers, gray wolves and exotic princes and princesses that you will see in the pages that follow.

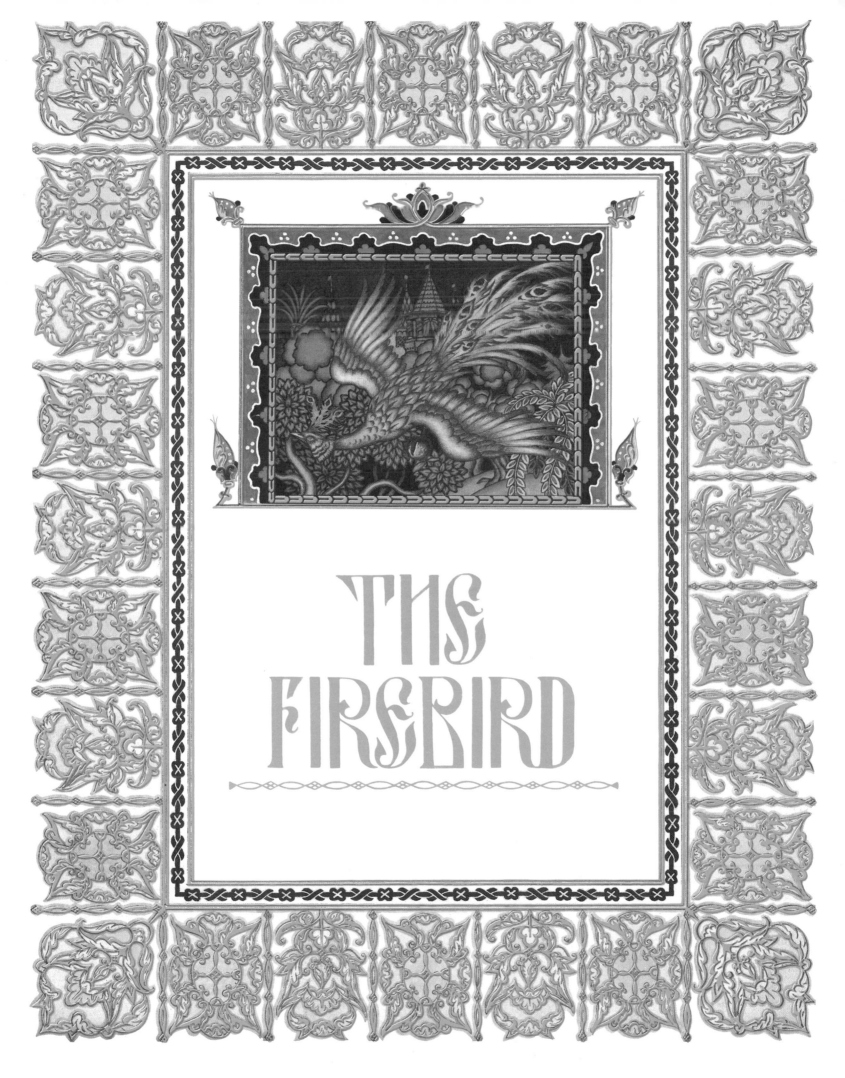

THE FIREBIRD

ong ago, in a distant kingdom, in a distant land, lived Tsar Vyslav Andronovich. He had three sons: the first was Tsarevich Dimitri, the second Tsarevich Vassili, and the third Tsarevich Ivan. Tsar Vyslav Andronovich had a garden so magnificent that there was no finer one in any kingdom. In this garden grew precious trees, with and without fruit. One special apple tree was the Tsar's favorite, for it bore only golden apples.

A firebird began to visit the garden of Tsar Vyslav; her wings were golden and her eyes were like Oriental crystals. Every night she flew down and alighted on Tsar Vyslav's favorite apple tree, plucked some golden apples, then flew away.

Tsar Vyslav Andronovich was greatly distressed at losing all the golden apples from his favorite tree. He summoned his three sons and said to them:

"My beloved children, which one of you can catch the firebird in my garden? To him who catches her alive, I will give half my kingdom during my life, and all of it upon my death."

His sons, the Tsareviches, answered with one voice:

"Gracious Sovereign, Little Father, Your Royal Majesty! With great joy will we try to take the firebird alive!"

The first night Tsarevich Dimitri went to keep watch in the garden. He waited under the golden apple tree, fell asleep, and did not hear the firebird fly in and pick many apples.

In the morning Tsar Vyslav Andronovich summoned his son the Tsarevich Dimitri to him and asked:

"My beloved son, did you see the firebird or not?"

"No, my Gracious Sovereign, Little Father, she did not come last night."

The second night Tsarevich Vassili went to the garden to keep watch for the firebird. He sat beneath the same apple tree, and after one hour he fell asleep so soundly that he did not hear the firebird come and pluck the golden apples.

In the morning Tsar Vyslav Andronovich summoned his son Tsarevich Vassili and asked:

"My beloved son, did you see the firebird or not?"

"Gracious Sovereign, Little Father, she did not come last night!"

The third night Tsarevich Ivan went to keep watch in the garden and sat under the same apple tree. He sat one hour, a second hour, and a third. Suddenly, the whole garden was lighted as if by many torches. The firebird came flying in, perched on the apple tree, and began to peck off apples. Tsarevich Ivan stole up to her so softly that he was able to seize her by the tail. But he could not hold her; she flew away, and Tsarevich Ivan was left with nothing but a tail-feather in his hand.

In the morning, as soon as Tsar Vyslav was awake, Tsarevich Ivan went to him and gave him the tailfeather of the firebird. This feather was so marvelous and so luminous that it lit up the dark chamber like bright sunlight.

Tsar Vyslav summoned his sons once again and said to them: ◆◆◆

"My beloved children, set out. I give you my blessing. Find the firebird and bring her to me alive, and that which I promised before, he who brings me the firebird will receive."

The Tsareviches Dimitri and Vassili bore a grudge against their youngest brother, Tsarevich Ivan, because he had succeeded in tearing a feather from the firebird's tail; they accepted their father's blessing and went forth together to seek the firebird. Tsarevich Ivan begged for his father's blessing also. Tsar Vyslav tried to hold Tsarevich Ivan back, but he finally had to yield to his son's insistent pleas.

Tsarevich Ivan accepted his father's blessing, chose a horse, and set out on his way, not knowing whither he was going. He rode near and far, high and low, until he came to a wide green field in the open countryside. In the field there stood a column and on the column these words were written: ◆◆◆

"He who travels from the column on the road straight ahead will be cold and hungry; he who travels to the right will be safe and sound, but his horse will be killed; and he who travels to the left will be killed, but his horse will be safe and sound."

Tsarevich Ivan read this inscription and rode to the right with the thought

"Find the firebird and bring her to me alive. . . ."

14

that if his horse were to die, at least he would remain alive.

He rode one day, a second day and a third. Suddenly he met a very large gray wolf who said to him: ❖❖❖

"Ah, it is you, young lad, Tsarevich Ivan! Did you not read what is written on the column, that your horse will be killed? Then why have you come this way?" The wolf spoke these words, then tore Tsarevich Ivan's horse in two and ran off into the countryside.

Tsarevich Ivan wept bitterly for his horse and set out on foot. He walked for a whole day and was very tired. He was about to sit down and rest when suddenly the gray wolf caught up with him and said: ❖❖❖

"I feel sorry for you, Tsarevich Ivan, because you are exhausted from walking. Climb on me, the gray wolf, and tell me where you wish to go, and why." Tsarevich Ivan told the gray wolf what errand he had come on, and the gray wolf galloped off with him more swiftly than a horse, and after some time, just at nightfall, brought him to a low stone wall, stopped, and said: ❖❖❖

"Now, Tsarevich Ivan, climb down from me, the gray wolf, and climb over that stone wall. Behind the wall you will find a garden, and in the garden is the firebird in a golden cage. Take the firebird, but leave the golden cage; if you take the cage you will be caught at once!"

Tsarevich Ivan climbed over the stone wall into the garden, saw the firebird in the golden cage, and was charmed by her. He took the firebird from the cage and started back, but on his way he said to himself, "Why have I taken the firebird without her cage? Where will I put her?" He returned, but as soon as he touched the cage there was a thunderous noise in the garden, for the cage was attached to ropes.

The guards awoke, ran into the garden, seized Tsarevich Ivan, and brought him before their Tsar, who was named Dolmat.

Tsar Dolmat flew into a rage against Tsarevich Ivan and cried in a loud, harsh voice: ❖❖❖

"Are you not ashamed to steal, young man? Who are you, from what land do you come, who is your father, and what is your name?"

Tsarevich Ivan answered: ❖❖❖

"I am the son of Tsar Vyslav Andronovich and my name is Tsarevich Ivan. Your firebird has been visiting our garden night after night, picking golden apples from my father's favorite tree. For that reason my father has sent me to find the firebird and bring her to him."

"Oh, young lad, Tsarevich Ivan," said Tsar Dolmat, "is it proper to do what you have done? If you had come to me, I would have given you the firebird. But now, will you like it if I proclaim in all lands how dishonorably you have entered my kingdom? However, listen, Tsarevich Ivan. If you will do me a service, if you will go to the ends of the earth and bring me back the horse with the golden mane from the realm of Tsar Afron, I will pardon your offense and give you the firebird with great pleasure."

Tsarevich Ivan left Tsar Dolmat sadly. He went to the gray wolf, and told him what Tsar Dolmat had said.

"Oh, young lad, Tsarevich Ivan," said the gray wolf, "why did you not listen to me and why did you take the golden cage?"

"It is true; I am guilty!" answered Tsarevich Ivan.

"Well, let it be so," said the gray wolf, "climb on me, on the gray wolf. I will carry you where you must go."

Tsarevich Ivan climbed onto the gray wolf's back and the wolf ran, as fast as an arrow. He ran for a long time or a short time, until at nightfall he came to the kingdom of Tsar Afron. When they reached the white-walled royal stables, the gray wolf said to Tsarevich Ivan:

"Step into those white-walled stables and take the horse with the golden mane. However, on the wall there hangs a golden bridle. Do not take it or misfortune will come to you."

Tsarevich Ivan entered the white-walled stables, took the horse, and started back. But on the wall he saw the golden bridle, and was so charmed by it that he lifted it from its nail.

No sooner had he touched it than a thunderous noise resounded through the stables, because it was attached to ropes. The stable boys and guard awoke, rushed in, searched Tsarevich Ivan, and brought him before Tsar Afron.

Tsar Afron began to question him:

"Young lad, tell me from what kingdom do you come, who is your father, and what is your name?"

Tsarevich Ivan answered:

"I am the son of Tsar Vyslav Andronovich, and I am called Tsarevich Ivan."

"Oh, young lad, Tsarevich Ivan," said Tsar Afron, "is the deed you have done worthy of an honorable knight? If you had come to me I would have gladly given you the horse with the golden mane. But now, will you like it if I send word to all the kingdoms to proclaim how dishonorably you have behaved in my kingdom? However, listen, Tsarevich Ivan. If you do me the service of going to the ends of earth to bring me the royal Tsarevna Elena the Fair, whom I have long loved with heart and soul, but whom I cannot win for my bride, I

Sitting on the gray wolf with the beautiful Tsarevna Elena the Fair. . . .

will gladly give you the horse with the golden mane and the golden bridle, and will forgive you your offense. If you do not perform this service for me, I will let it be known in all the kingdoms that you are a thief without honor!"

Tsarevich Ivan left the palace and began weeping bitterly. He came to the gray wolf and told him all that had happened.

"Oh, young lad, Tsarevich Ivan," said the gray wolf, "why did you not listen to me? Why did you take the golden bridle?"

"I am guilty before you," answered Tsarevich Ivan.

"Well, let it be so," said the gray wolf. "Climb on me, on the gray wolf. I will take you where you must go!"

Tsarevich Ivan climbed on the gray wolf's back and the wolf ran as fast as an arrow until he arrived in the kingdom of the royal Tsarevna Elena the Fair. When they came to a golden fence surrounding a beautiful garden, the wolf said to Tsarevich Ivan: ❖❖❖

"Now, Tsarevich Ivan, climb down from me, from the gray wolf, and go back along the same road that we took to come here, and wait for me in the open field under the green oak."

Tsarevich Ivan went where he was bid.

The gray wolf sat near the golden fence and waited for Tsarevna Elena the Fair to come to the garden. Toward evening, as the sun began to set in the west, Tsarevna Elena the Fair came to walk in the garden with her servants and governesses and ladies-in-waiting. When she came to the place where the gray wolf was sitting behind the fence, he quickly jumped over the fence into the garden, seized the Tsarevna Elena the Fair, jumped back again, and ran off with her with all his strength. He came to the green oak in the open field where Tsarevich Ivan was waiting for him and said: ❖❖❖

"Tsarevich Ivan, climb quickly on me, on the gray wolf!"

Tsarevich Ivan climbed on him, and the gray wolf darted off with them both toward the kingdom of Tsar Afron.

The nurses and governesses and all the ladies-in-waiting ran at once to the palace and sent men-at-arms in pursuit, but no matter how fast they ran, they could not overtake the gray wolf, and so they turned back.

Sitting on the gray wolf with the beautiful Tsarevna Elena the Fair, Tsarevich Ivan came to love her with all his heart and she to love him. When the gray wolf reached the kingdom of Tsar Afron, Tsarevich Ivan became extremely sad and began to weep.

The gray wolf asked:

"Why are you weeping, Tsarevich Ivan?"

The Tsarevich answered:

"Gray wolf, my friend, why should I not weep and grieve? I love Tsarevna Elena with all my heart, and now I must give her to Tsar Afron in return for the horse with the golden mane. If I do not give her to him, he will dishonor me in all the kingdom!"

"I have served you well, Tsarevich Ivan," said the gray wolf, "and I will render you this further service. Listen to me, Tsarevich Ivan! I will turn myself into the beautiful Tsarevna Elena, and you will lead me to the Tsar and take the horse with the golden mane. He will think me the true Tsarevna, and when you have mounted the horse with the golden mane and ridden far away, I shall ask Tsar Afron to let me walk in the open field. When he lets me go with the nurses and governesses and ladies-in-waiting and I am with them in the open field, think of me, and once again I shall be with you."

The gray wolf spoke these words, hurled himself against the damp earth,

and turned into the Tsarevna Elena the Fair. Tsarevich Ivan led the gray wolf to the palace of Tsar Afron after telling Tsarevna Elena to wait for him outside the town. When Tsarevich Ivan came to Tsar Afron with the false Elena the Fair, the Tsar rejoiced to receive the treasure he had so long desired, and gave Tsarevich Ivan the horse with the golden mane.

Tsarevich Ivan mounted the horse and rode out of town. He seated Elena the Fair beside him and set out in the direction of the kingdom of Tsar Dolmat.

The gray wolf lived with Tsar Afron one day, a second day, and a third in place of Elena the Fair. On the fourth day he went to Tsar Afron and asked his permission to take a walk in the countryside to dispel his sadness.

Tsar Afron said to him:

"Ah, my beautiful Tsarevna Elena! I would do anything for you!" At once he ordered the governesses and nurses and all the ladies-in-waiting to walk with the Tsarevna in the countryside.

Meanwhile Tsarevich Ivan continued his journey with Elena the Fair. He conversed with her and forgot about the gray wolf, then suddenly he remembered:

"Oh, where are you, my gray wolf?"

Suddenly, from out of nowhere, the gray wolf appeared before Tsarevich Ivan and said, "Climb on me, Tsarevich Ivan, onto the gray wolf, and let the beautiful Tsarevna ride on the horse with the golden mane."

Tsarevich Ivan mounted the gray wolf and they continued their journey to the kingdom of Tsar Dolmat.

They traveled for a long time or a short time, and reaching the kingdom, they stopped three versts from the town. Tsarevich Ivan began to implore the gray wolf, saying:

"Listen to me, gray wolf, my dear friend. You have done me many a service, do me this last one. Could you not turn yourself into a horse with a golden mane, because I cannot bear to part from this one?"

Suddenly the gray wolf hurled himself against the damp earth and turned into a horse with a golden mane. Tsarevich Ivan left Tsarevna Elena the Fair in a green meadow, climbed onto the gray wolf, and set out for the court of Tsar Dolmat. When Tsar Dolmat saw Tsarevich Ivan riding on the false horse with the golden mane, he was overjoyed, and at once came out of his palace, met the Tsarevich Ivan in the great courtyard, kissed him on his sweet lips, took him by the right hand, led him into the white-walled palace, and in honor of the joyous occasion ordered a great feast prepared.

The guests sat at oaken tables with checked tablecloths. They ate, drank, laughed, and enjoyed themselves for two days, and on the third day Tsar Dolmat gave Tsarevich Ivan the firebird and the golden cage.

Then Tsarevich took the firebird, left the town, mounted the horse with the golden mane, and, with Tsarevna Elena the Fair, set out for his own country.

Tsar Dolmat the next day decided to take a ride in the countryside on his horse with the golden mane, but at once the horse bolted, threw Tsar Dolmat to the ground, turned back into the gray wolf, darted off, and overtook Tsarevich Ivan.

"Tsarevich Ivan," said he, "climb on me, the gray wolf, and let Tsarevna Elena the Fair ride the horse with the golden mane." The Tsarevich then sat on the gray wolf and they continued on their way.

When they came to the place where the wolf had torn Tsarevich Ivan's horse asunder, he stopped and said:

"Well, Tsarevich Ivan, I have served you long in faith and truth. Upon this spot I tore your horse in two and to this spot I have returned you safe and sound. Climb down from me, the gray wolf. Now you have a horse with a golden mane and you have no further need of me!"

After he had spoken these words, the gray wolf ran off into the countryside. Tsarevich Ivan wept bitterly and continued his journey with the beautiful Tsarevna.

He rode for a long time or a short time with Tsarevna Elena the Fair on the horse with the golden mane. When they were about twenty versts from his own land, he stopped, dismounted, and lay down to rest with the beautiful Tsarevna in the shade of a tree. He tied the horse with the golden mane to the tree and put the cage with the firebird by his side. They lay on the soft grass, spoke tender words to each other, and fell into a deep sleep.

At that very moment, Tsarevich Ivan's brothers, Tsarevich Dimitri and Tsarevich Vassili, having traveled through various kingdoms and having failed to find the firebird, were returning to their country empty-handed. They came by chance upon their brother, Tsarevich Ivan, sleeping beside Tsarevna Elena the Fair. Seeing the horse with the golden mane on the grass, and the firebird in the golden cage, they were sorely tempted and decided to slay their brother, Tsarevich Ivan.

Tsarevich Dimitri drew his sword from its scabbard and stabbed Tsarevich Ivan. Then he awakened Tsarevna Elena the Fair and asked her:

"Beautiful maiden, from what kingdom do you come? Who is your father and what is your name?"

Tsarevna Elena the Fair, seeing Tsarevich Ivan dead, was very frightened and began to weep bitter tears. She answered:

"I am the Tsar's daughter, Elena the Fair. I was carried off by Tsarevich

Ivan, whom you have so cruelly slain. If you were valiant knights, you would have gone with him into the countryside and conquered him in fair combat; but you slew him in his sleep. What praise will that win you, to kill a sleeping man?"

Tsarevich Dimitri put his sword to the heart of Tsarevna Elena and said to her:

"Listen to me, Elena the Fair! You are now in our hands. We will take you to our father, Tsar Vyslav Andronovich, and you must tell him that we captured you with the firebird and the horse with the golden mane. If you do not promise to say that, we shall put you to death at once."

Tsarevna Elena the Fair, frightened by the threat of death, promised them, and swore by everything sacred that she would speak as they commanded.

The Tsarevich Dimitri and Tsarevich Vassili cast lots to see who should get Tsarevna Elena and who the horse with the golden mane. And it fell out that Tsarevna Elena went to Tsarevich Vassili and the horse with the golden mane to Tsarevich Dimitri.

Tsarevich Ivan lay dead upon the ground for thirty days. Then the gray wolf came upon him and knew him by his odor; he wished to help him, to revive him, but he did not know how.

At that moment, the gray wolf saw a raven with two young ravens flying above the cadaver, making ready to swoop down and eat the flesh of Tsarevich Ivan. The gray wolf hid behind a bush, and as soon as the young ravens alighted and began to eat the body of Tsarevich Ivan, he leaped out, caught one young raven, and prepared to tear him in two. The mother raven flew to the ground, sat at some distance from the gray wolf and said:

"Oh, be praised, gray wolf! Do not harm my child; he has done nothing to you!"

"Listen, raven, child of raven," answered the gray wolf, "I shall not touch your young one, if you will do me a service. Fly to the ends of the earth and bring me back the water of death and the water of life!"

At this, the raven answered the gray wolf:

"I will do you this service, only do not harm my child." The raven spoke these words and flew off.

On the third day the raven returned carrying two vials, one containing the water of life, the other the water of death, and gave them to the gray wolf. The gray wolf took the vials, tore the little raven in two, sprinkled it with the water of death, and the young raven's body grew together. He sprinkled it with the water of life and it flapped its wings and flew away.

Then the gray wolf sprinkled Tsarevich Ivan with the water of death. His body grew together. He sprinkled him with the water of life. Tsarevich Ivan stood up and said:

"Ah, what a long time I have slept here."

At this, the gray wolf answered:

"Without me, Tsarevich Ivan, you would have slept forever. Know that your brothers stabbed you and carried off Tsarevna Elena the Fair, the horse with the golden mane, and the firebird. Now, hasten as fast as you can to your native land. Your brother, Tsarevich Vassili, is this very day to marry your fiancée, the beautiful Tsarevna Elena. To get there quickly, climb on me, the gray wolf!"

Tsarevich Ivan climbed onto the gray wolf. The wolf ran with him to the kingdom of Tsar Vyslav Andronovich, and after a long time or a short time reached the town.

Tsarevich Ivan dismounted from the gray wolf, entered the town, and,

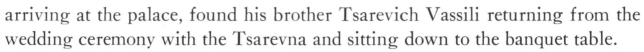

arriving at the palace, found his brother Tsarevich Vassili returning from the wedding ceremony with the Tsarevna and sitting down to the banquet table.

As soon as Elena the Fair saw Tsarevich Ivan, she sprang up and began to kiss his sweet lips and cried out:

"This is my beloved bridegroom, Tsarevich Ivan, not the scoundrel who sits here at this table."

Then Tsar Vyslav Andronovich arose from his place and began to question Tsarevna Elena the Fair:

"What is the meaning of the words you have spoken?"

Elena the Fair told him the whole truth about all that had happened. Tsar Vyslav was enraged with his sons Dimitri and Vassili and had them thrown into a dungeon.

Tsarevich Ivan married Tsarevna Elena the Fair and lived with her in such friendship and such love that neither could bear to be parted from the other for as much as a single moment.

MARIA MOREVNA

<u>Firebird</u> grey wolf Ivan + Tsarevitch
"horse Tsar Tsale
"well, let it be so.
Ivan's corpse smells.

Maria Morevna - forgive me for lookg
into room + releasing Kostchey
(Tsarevitch 'sat on a stone + wept.'

<u>The snow maiden</u> - melts
Kupava throws herself into
well

<u>Vassilissa</u> stepmother worked her
to make her Hm + ugly (but her
+ daughters > ")
doll did her work + herb agamst
sunburn. Practical tasks for
all 3 + reason for V. to go to
Baba Yaga.   Stepmother +
daughters d. V buries skull,
stays w. old woman - wants to

latest ~~cream~~ (~~feet~~)

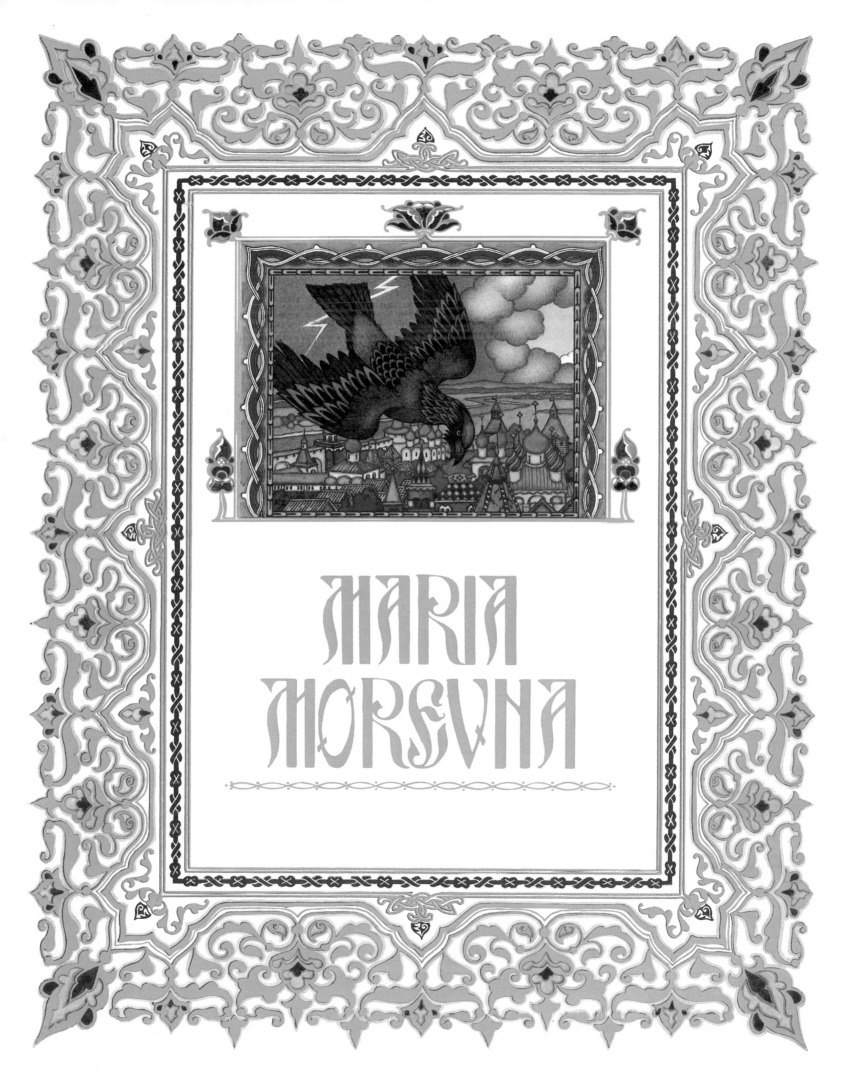

MARIA
MOREVNA

n a certain kingdom in a certain land there lived the young Tsarevich Ivan. He had three sisters: Tsarevna Maria, Tsarevna Olga, and Tsarevna Anna.

Their father and mother lay dying; on the point of death they said to their son:

"Give your sisters in marriage to the first person who comes to ask for their hands, but do not let him stay for long."

Tsarevich Ivan buried his parents, and with a heavy heart went to walk with his sisters in a green garden. Suddenly a black cloud covered the sky and a terrible storm arose.

"Sisters, let us return home!" said Tsarevich Ivan. They reached the palace just as the thunder rumbled. The sky split in two and a white falcon flew toward them; the falcon fell to earth, turned into a handsome youth, and said:

"Good morning, Tsarevich Ivan. I used to come here as a guest; now I come as a suitor. I wish to take Tsarevna Maria as my bride."

"If my sister loves you, I will not stop her. Let her go with God."

Tsarevna Maria agreed. The falcon married her and took her off to his kingdom.

Day followed day; hour followed hour. A whole year quickly passed. Tsarevich Ivan went walking with his two sisters in a green garden. Once again a storm came up, a whirlwind with lightning. "Let us return home, sisters," said Tsarevich Ivan. They reached the palace just as the thunder cracked. The palace roof was shattered, the sky split in two, and an eagle flew down. The eagle fell to earth and turned into a handsome youth.

"Good morning, Tsarevich Ivan. I used to come here as a guest; now I come as a suitor!" And he asked for Tsarevna Olga in marriage.

Tsarevich Ivan answered:

"If you are loved by Tsarevna Olga, she may go with you; I will not deprive her of her freedom."

Tsarevna Olga agreed and married the eagle. The eagle took her away to his kingdom.

Another year passed. The Tsarevich said to his youngest sister: "Let us go for a walk in the green garden." They walked for a little while, and once again a storm came up, a whirlwind with lightning. "Let us return home, little sister."

They returned to the palace, and before they could sit down the thunder rumbled and opened the sky. A raven flew down, fell to earth, and turned into a handsome youth. He was even more pleasing than the first two.

"Well, Tsarevich Ivan! I used to come here as a guest; now I come as a suitor. Give me Tsarevna Anna!"

"I will not go against my sister's wishes. If she loves you, let her go with you."

Tsarevna Anna left with the raven, and he took her away to his kingdom.

Tsarevich Ivan was left alone. For one whole year he lived without his sisters and grew restless. One day he said: ❖❖❖

"I shall go and find a sister."

He set off, and on his way came upon a mighty host, lying vanquished in a field. Tsarevich Ivan called out: ❖❖❖

"If any man there is alive, let him answer me! Who has massacred this great army?"

One man still alive answered his call: ❖❖❖

"Maria Morevna, the beautiful Tsarevna, has vanquished this great army!"

Tsarevich Ivan ventured farther until he came upon white tents. Maria Morevna came out to meet him.

"Good morning, Tsarevich, where is God taking you? Do you come at your will or against your will?"

Tsarevich Ivan answered: ❖❖❖

"Brave men do not go about against their will!"

"Well then, if you are not in a hurry, come and pay me a visit in my tent."

Tsarevich Ivan was pleased. He passed two nights in the tent, was loved by Maria Morevna, and married her.

Maria Morevna, the beautiful Tsarevna, took him with her to her kingdom. They lived together for a while; then the princess decided to prepare for war. She left her household in charge of Tsarevich Ivan and said to him: ❖❖❖

Tsarevich Ivan ventured farther until he came upon white tents. Maria Morevna came out to meet him.

34

"Go everywhere, watch over everything. Only do not look into that chamber!"

He could not resist; as soon as Maria Morevna was gone, he ran to the chamber, threw open the door, and looked in. There hung Koshchey the Deathless, chained with a dozen chains. Koshchey begged Tsarevich Ivan:

"Have pity on me; help me! For ten years I have been tortured here. I have neither eaten nor drunk. My throat is completely parched."

The Tsarevich gave him a full pitcher of wine; he drank it and demanded more.

"One pitcher of wine cannot quench my thirst; give me another!"

The Tsarevich gave him another pitcher; Koshchey drank it and demanded a third, and when he had drunk three pitchers he regained his strength, rattled his chains, and suddenly burst all twelve.

"Many thanks, Tsarevich Ivan," said Koshchey the Deathless. "Now you will never see Maria Morevna except with your ears!" Like a great whirlwind he flew from the window, overtook Maria Morevna, the beautiful Tsarevna, seized her, and carried her off with him.

Tsarevich Ivan wept bitterly, bitterly. Then he made ready and set out.

"Whatever happens, I will search for Maria Morevna!"

He rode one day, he rode a second day. At twilight on the third day he saw a beautiful castle; by the castle stood an oak tree and on the oak tree sat a white falcon. The falcon flew down from the oak, fell to earth, changed into a handsome youth, and cried:

"Ah, my dear brother-in-law! May the Lord give you grace!"

Tsarevna Maria came running. She welcomed Tsarevich Ivan with joy, questioned him about his health, and told him of her life.

The Tsarevich stayed three days with them, then said:

"I can stay with you no longer. I must go in search of my wife, Maria Morevna, the beautiful Tsarevna!"

"It will be hard to find her," answered the falcon. "Leave us at least your silver spoon. We will look at it and remember you!"

Tsarevich Ivan left his silver spoon with the falcon and set out again.

He rode one day, he rode a second day. At twilight on the third day he saw a castle more beautiful than the first. By the castle stood an oak tree; on the oak tree sat an eagle. The eagle flew down from the tree, fell to earth, turned into a handsome youth, and cried:

"Come, Tsarevna Olga, our dear brother has arrived!"

Tsarevna Olga ran to him, kissed him, embraced him, questioned him about his health, and told him of her life.

Tsarevich Ivan stayed three days with them, then said:

"I can stay with you no longer; I must go in search of my wife, Maria Morevna, the beautiful Tsarevna."

The eagle answered:

"It will be hard to find her. Leave us at least your silver fork. We will look at it and remember you!"

He left his silver fork and set out again.

One day passed; a second day passed. At twilight on the third day he saw a castle more beautiful than the first two. By the castle stood an oak tree; on the oak tree perched a raven. The raven flew down from the oak tree, came to earth, turned into a handsome youth, and cried:

"Tsarevna Anna, come quickly, our brother is here!" Tsarevna Anna came running, welcomed him with joy, kissed him, embraced him, questioned him about his health, and told him of her life.

Tsarevich Ivan stayed three days with them, then said:

"Farewell! I must search for my wife, Maria Morevna, the beautiful Tsarevna!"

The raven answered:

"It will be hard to find her. Leave us at least your silver snuff box. We will look at it and think of you!"

Tsarevich Ivan gave them his silver snuff box, bade them farewell, and set out again.

One day passed, a second day passed. On the third day he caught up with Maria Morevna. She saw her beloved, threw her arms around him, burst into tears, and said:

"Ah, Tsarevich Ivan, why did you not listen to me? Why did you look into the chamber and why did you let Koshchey the Deathless escape?"

"Forgive me, Maria Morevna! Forget the past! Leave with me now, while we cannot see Koshchey the Deathless. Perhaps he will not catch up with us!" They made ready and set off.

Koshchey was out hunting. Toward evening he started home. Suddenly his horse snorted.

"Why do you snort, starving beast? Do you smell danger?"

The horse answered:

"Tsarevich Ivan has been here. He has taken Maria Morevna!"

"Can we catch up with them?"

"We can sow wheat, wait till it grows tall, harvest it, thresh it, turn it into

Like a great whirlwind he flew from the window, overtook
Maria Morevna . . . and carried her off with him.

38

flour, bake five ovens full of bread, eat the bread, then set out in pursuit and still catch them in time!"

Koshchey started off at a gallop. He caught up with Tsarevich Ivan.

"See here," he said, "I will pardon you once for your kindness of heart, because you gave me to drink. I will pardon you a second time. But the third time, beware, for I shall chop you in pieces." He seized Maria Morevna and carried her off, and Tsarevich Ivan sat on a stone and began to weep.

He wept and he wept and turned back once again after Maria Morevna. Koshchey the Deathless was not at home.

"Let us flee, Maria Morevna!"

"Ah, Tsarevich Ivan, he will follow us!"

"Let him follow! At least we will spend another hour together!"

They made ready and set out.

Koshchey the Deathless was returning home. Suddenly his horse snorted.

"Why do you snort, starving beast? Do you smell danger?"

"Tsarevich Ivan has come. He has taken Maria Morevna away!"

"Can we catch up with them?"

"We can sow barley, wait till it grows tall, harvest it, thresh it, make beer, drink until drunk, sleep off our drunkenness, then set out in pursuit and still catch them in time!"

Koshchey started off at a gallop. He caught up with Tsarevich Ivan.

"Have I not already told you that you shall never again see Maria Morevna, except with your ears?" He seized Maria Morevna and carried her off.

Tsarevich Ivan was alone. He wept and turned back once again after Maria Morevna.

Koshchey was not at home.

"Let us flee, Maria Morevna."

"Ah, Tsarevich Ivan! You know he will catch us and chop you to pieces!"

"Let him chop me! I cannot live without you!"

They made ready and set out.

Koshchey the Deathless was returning home. Suddenly his horse snorted.

"Why are you snorting? Do you smell danger?"

"Tsarevich Ivan has come. He has taken Maria Morevna away!" Koshchey started off at a gallop; he caught up with Tsarevich Ivan, chopped him in pieces, and put him in a wine cask. He bound the cask with hoops of iron and threw it into the blue sea. Then he took Maria Morevna to his house.

Meanwhile, the brothers-in-law saw their silver turning black. "Ah!" said they. "Something evil has happened!"

The eagle flew over the blue sea. He seized the wine cask and dragged it to shore. The falcon flew to the water of life and the raven to the water of death. They swerved down in a row, tore open the cask, took out the pieces of Tsarevich Ivan, washed them, and put them in place. The raven sprinkled them with the water of death; the pieces of the cadaver united. The falcon sprinkled them with the water of life. Tsarevich Ivan, shivered, stood up and said: ❖❖❖

"Ah! How long I have slept!"

"You would have slept longer without us!" answered the brothers-in-law. "Come now and visit us."

"No, brothers, I must search for Maria Morevna!"

He found her and said, "Find out from Koshchey the Deathless where he got such a fine horse!"

Maria Morevna waited for the right moment, then began to question Koshchey. Koshchey answered: ❖❖❖

"In a faraway land, behind a river of fire, lives Baba Yaga. She has another such mare, on which she flies around the earth every day. She has many excellent mares; once I was a pasture-boy there for three days. I did not let a single mare escape, and for that, Baba Yaga gave me a colt."

"How did you cross the river of fire?"

"I have a handkerchief. When I wave it to the right, it becomes a high, high bridge that the fire cannot reach."

Maria Morevna listened, told Tsarevich Ivan, took the handkerchief, and gave it to him.

Tsarevich Ivan crossed the river of fire and made his way toward Baba Yaga. He went for a long time without drinking or eating. He met a bird from across the sea, with her young. Tsarevich Ivan said: ❖❖❖

"I would gladly eat a little bird!"

"Do not eat me, Tsarevich Ivan," said the exotic bird. "No matter when, I will serve you!"

He went farther. In a forest he saw a beehive.

"I would gladly eat some honey!" he said.

"Do not touch my honey, Tsarevich Ivan. No matter when, I will serve you!"

"Good, let it be at your will."

He did not touch the honey and went farther. He met a lioness with her cub.

"I would gladly eat that lion cub. I am so hungry that I feel ill."

"Do not touch my cub, Tsarevich Ivan," begged the lioness. "No matter when, I will serve you!"

On the third day he saw a castle more beautiful than the first.

"Good, let it be at your will."

He continued slowly, on and on. The house of Baba Yaga appeared. Around the house were twelve spikes, and on eleven of these spikes was the head of a man. The last spike was bare.

"Good morning, Grandmother!"

"Good morning, Tsarevich Ivan! Do you come in good will or by force?"

"I have come to win from you a powerful horse!"

"Certainly, Tsarevich! I will not oblige you to serve a year, but only three days. If you guard my mares with care, I will give you a powerful horse. If not, I will display your head on that last spike!"

Tsarevich Ivan agreed. Baba Yaga gave him food and drink and ordered him to set to work.

No sooner had he let the mares loose in the countryside than they put their tails in the air and galloped away on all sides over the fields. The Tsarevich could not see where they had fled. He began to weep, to despair. He sat on a stone and fell asleep. The sun was setting when the exotic bird came flying and woke him up:

"Wake up, Tsarevich Ivan! The mares have gone back to the house!"

The Tsarevich awoke and returned to the house, where Baba Yaga was making noise and shouting at her mares:

"Why have you all come home?"

"Why should we not come home? Birds came flying at us from all sides, trying to peck out our eyes!"

"Very well, tomorrow you will not run in the fields, you will scatter into the deep forest!"

Tsarevich Ivan slept through the night. In the morning Baba Yaga said to him:

"Watch out, Tsarevich! If you do not guard my mares well, if you lose just one of them, your audacious head will be stuck on that spike!"

He led the mares into the countryside. At once, they put their tails in the air and fled. Once again the Tsarevich sat on a stone. He wept and wept, and fell asleep. The sun set beyond the forest. A lioness came running.

"Wake up, Tsarevich Ivan, all the mares are back together!"

Tsarevich Ivan got up and returned to the house. Baba Yaga was making more noise than the first time, shouting at her mares.

"Why have you all come home?"

"Why should we not come home? Ferocious beasts sprang on us from everywhere. They nearly tore us to pieces!"

"Very well, tomorrow you will swim off into the blue sea!"

Once again Tsarevich Ivan slept through the night. In the morning Baba Yaga sent him to pasture her mares.

"If you do not guard them with care, your audacious head will be stuck on that spike!"

He drove the mares into the countryside. At once, they put their tails in the air, disappeared from sight, and plunged up to their necks in the blue sea. Tsarevich Ivan sat on a stone, wept, and fell asleep. The sun set beyond the forest. A bee flew toward him and said:

"Wake up, Tsarevich Ivan! The mares are back together. When you go back to the house, do not let Baba Yaga see you. Go into the stable and hide behind the corncribs. There you will find a mangy colt resting on the dung.

Steal him, and on the stroke of midnight, flee!"

Tsarevich Ivan got up, slipped into the stable, and hid behind the corncribs. Baba Yaga was making noise, shouting at her mares:

"Why have you all come back?"

"Why should we not come back? A great swarm of bees surrounded us and stung us until they drew blood!"

Baba Yaga slept, and that same night Tsarevich Ivan stole her mangy colt, saddled it, mounted it, and galloped toward the river of fire. At the river's edge he shook his handkerchief three times to the right, and suddenly there appeared, arching over the river, a high, solid bridge. The Tsarevich crossed the bridge and shook his handkerchief to the left twice only. The bridge grew thinner and thinner over the river.

In the morning Baba Yaga awoke and missed her mangy colt. She set out in pursuit. She galloped at full speed in her iron mortar, thrusting with her iron pestle, brushing her tracks away with her broom.

She galloped up to the river of fire, looked and thought: "What a beautiful bridge!"

She started over the bridge. When she reached the middle, the bridge broke and Baba Yaga fell into the river, there to meet a horrible death.

Tsarevich Ivan fattened the colt in the green fields until it grew into a splendid horse. He returned to Maria Morevna. She ran toward him and threw her arms around his neck.

"God has revived you!"

"So He has," said he. "Come with me!"

"Beware, Tsarevich Ivan! If Koshchey catches you, he will chop you in pieces again!"

"He will not catch me. Now I have a powerful horse; he flies like a bird!" They mounted the horse and sped away.

Koshchey the Deathless returned to his house. His horse snorted beneath him.

"What is the matter, starving beast? Do you smell danger?"

"Tsarevich Ivan has come and carried off Maria Morevna!"

"Can we catch them?"

"God knows. Now Tsarevich Ivan has a powerful horse, better than me!"

"No matter, I must pursue him!" said Koshchey the Deathless.

After a long time or a short time he caught up with Tsarevich Ivan and jumped to the ground to chop him in pieces with his curved sword. But Tsarevich Ivan's horse kicked Koshchey the Deathless with all its might and clove in his skull, and the Tsarevich beat him to death with his club.

Then the Tsarevich gathered wood, set it on fire, burned Koshchey the Deathless on the pyre, and scattered his ashes to the wind.

Maria Morevna mounted the horse of Koshchey the Deathless, Tsarevich Ivan mounted his own, and they went to visit first the raven, then the eagle, then the falcon.

Wherever they went they were welcomed with joy.

"Ah! Tsarevich Ivan, we despaired of seeing you again. Your travels and troubles were not all in vain. You could search the world for a beauty like Maria Morevna and never find another as fair!"

They stayed for a while, joined in the feasts, then returned to their kingdom. There they lived in peace, amassing riches and drinking much wine.

THE
SNOW MAIDEN

THE SNOW
MAIDEN

nce upon a time there lived a woodcutter and his old wife. They were poor and had no children. The old man cut logs in the forest and carried them into town; in this way he eked out a living. As they grew older they became sadder and sadder at being childless.

"We are growing so old. Who will take care of us?" the wife would ask from time to time.

"Do not worry, old woman. God will not abandon us. He will come to our aid in time," answered the old man.

One day, in the dead of winter, he went into the forest to chop wood and his wife came along to help him. The cold was intense and they were nearly frozen.

"We have no child," said the woodcutter to his wife. "Shall we make a little snow girl to amuse us?"

They began to roll snowballs together, and in a short while they had made a "snegurochka," a snow maiden, so beautiful that no pen could describe her. The old man and the old woman gazed at her and grew even sadder.

"If only the good Lord had sent us a little girl to share our old age!" said the old woman

They thought on this so strongly that suddenly a miracle happened. They looked at their snow maiden, and were amazed at what they saw. The eyes of the snow maiden twinkled; a diadem studded with precious stones sparkled like fire on her head; a cape of brocade covered her shoulders; embroidered boots appeared on her feet.

The old couple looked at her and did not believe their eyes. Then the mist of a breath parted the red lips of Snegurochka; she trembled, looked around, and took a step forward.

The old couple stood there, stupefied; they thought they were dreaming. Snegurochka came toward them and said: ❖❖❖

"Good day, kind folk, do not be frightened! I will be a good daughter to you, the joy of your old age. I will honor you as father and mother."

"My darling daughter, let it be as you desire," answered the old man. "Come home with us, our longed-for little girl!" They took her by her white hands and led her from the forest.

As they went, the pine trees swayed goodbye, saying their farewell to Snegurochka, with their rustling wishing her safe journey, happy life.

The old couple brought Snegurochka home to their wooden hut, their "isba," and she began her life with them, helping them to do the chores. She was always most respectful, she never contradicted them, and they could not praise her enough, nor tire of gazing at her, she was so kind and so beautiful.

Snegurochka, nevertheless, worried her adopted parents. She was not at all talkative and her little face was always pale, so pale. She did not seem to have a drop of blood, yet her eyes shone like little stars. And her smile! When she smiled she lighted up the isba like a gift of rubles!

They lived together thus for one month, two months; time passed. The old couple could not rejoice enough in their little daughter, gift of God.

One day the old woman said to Snegurochka:

"My darling daughter, why are you so shy? You see no friends, you always stay with us, old people; that must be tiresome for you. Why do you not go out and play with your friends, show yourself and see people? You should not spend all your time with us, aged folk."

"I have no wish to go out, dear Mother," answered Snegurochka. "I am happy here."

Carnival time arrived. The streets were alive with strollers, with singing from early morning until late at night. Snegurochka watched the merrymaking through the little frozen window panes. She watched . . . and finally she could resist no longer; she gave in to the old woman, put on her little cape, and went into the street to join the throng.

In the same village there lived a maiden called Kupava. She was a true beauty, with hair as black as a raven's wing, skin like blood and milk, and arching brows.

One day a rich merchant came through town. His name was Mizgir, and he was young and tall. He saw Kupava and she pleased him. Kupava was not at all shy; she was saucy and never turned down an invitation to stroll.

Mizgir stopped in the village, called to all the young girls, gave them nuts

and spiced bread, and danced with Kupava. From that moment he never left town, and, it must be said, he soon became Kupava's lover. There was Kupava, the belle of the town, parading about in velvets and silks, serving sweet wines to the youths and the maidens and living the joyful life.

The day Snegurochka first strolled in the street, she met Kupava, who introduced all her friends. From then on Snegurochka came out more often and looked at the youths. A young boy, a shepherd, pleased her. He was named Lel. Snegurochka pleased him too, and they became inseparable. Whenever the young girls came out to stroll and to sing, Lel would run to Snegurochka's isba, tap on the window, and say: ❖❖❖

"Snegurochka, dearest, come out and join the dancing." Once she appeared, he never left her side.

One day Mizgir came to the village as the maidens were dancing in the street. He joined in with Kupava and made them all laugh. He noticed Snegurochka and she pleased him; she was so pale and so pretty! From then on Kupava seemed to him too dark and too heavy. Soon he found her unpleasant. Quarrels and scenes broke out between them, and Mizgir stopped seeing her.

Kupava was desolate, but what could she do? One cannot please by force nor revive the past! She noticed that Mizgir often returned to the village and went to the house of Snegurochka's old parents. The rumor flew that Mizgir had asked for Snegurochka's hand in marriage.

When Kupava learned this, her heart trembled. She ran to Snegurochka's isba, reproached her, insulted her, called her a viper, a traitor, made such a scene that they had to force her to leave.

"I will go to the Tsar!" she cried. "I will not suffer this dishonor. There is

Tsar Berendei . . . sat erect on his gilded and sculptured throne.

no law that allows a man to compromise a maiden, then throw her aside like a useless rag!"

So Kupava went to the Tsar to beg for his help against Snegurochka, who she insisted had stolen her lover.

Tsar Berendei ruled this kingdom; he was a good and gracious Tsar who loved truth and watched over all his subjects. He listened to Kupava and ordered Snegurochka brought before him.

The Tsar's envoys arrived at the village with a proclamation ordering Snegurochka to appear before their master.

"Good subjects of the Tsar! Listen well and tell us where the maiden Snegurochka lives. The Tsar summons her! Let her make ready in haste! If she does not come of her will we will take her by force!"

The old woodcutters were filled with fear. But the Tsar's word was law. They helped Snegurochka to make ready and decided to accompany her, to present her to the Tsar.

Tsar Berendei lived in a splendid palace with walls of massive oak and wrought-iron doors; a large stairway led to great halls where Bukhara carpets covered the floors and guardsmen stood in scarlet kaftans with shining axes. All the vast courtyard was filled with people.

Once inside the sumptuous palace, the old couple and Snegurochka stood amazed. The ceilings and arches were covered with paintings, the precious plate was lined up on shelves, along the walls ran benches covered with carpets and brocades, and on these benches were seated the boyars wearing tall hats of bear fur trimmed with gold. Musicians played intricate music on their tympanums. At the far end of the hall, Tsar Berendei himself sat erect on his gilded and sculptured throne. Around him stood bodyguards in kaftans white as snow, holding silver axes.

Tsar Berendei's long white beard fell to his belt. His fur hat was the tallest; his kaftan of precious brocade was embroidered all over with jewels and with gold.

Snegurochka was frightened; she did not dare to take a step nor raise her eyes.

Tsar Berendei said to her: ❖❖❖

"Come here, young maiden, come closer, gentle Snegurochka. Do not be afraid, answer my questions. Did you commit the sin of separating two lovers, after stealing the heart of Kupava's beloved? Did you flirt with him and do you intend to marry him? Make sure that you tell me the truth!"

Snegurochka approached the Tsar, curtsied low, knelt before him, and spoke the truth; that she was not at fault, neither in body nor in soul; that it was true that the merchant Mizgir had asked for her in marriage, but that he did not please her and she had refused his hand.

Tsar Berendei took Snegurochka's hands to help her to rise, looked into her eyes and said: ❖❖❖

"I see in your eyes, lovely maiden, that you speak the truth, that you are nowhere at fault. Go home now in peace and do not be upset!"

And the Tsar let Snegurochka leave with her adoptive parents.

When Kupava learned of the Tsar's decision, she went wild with grief. She ripped her sarafan, tore her pearl necklace from her white neck, ran from her isba, and threw herself in the well.

From that day on, Snegurochka grew sadder and sadder. She no longer went

out in the street to stroll, not even when Lel begged her to come.

Meanwhile, spring had returned. The glorious sun rose higher and higher, the snow melted, the tender grass sprouted, the bushes turned green, the birds sang and made their nests. But the more the sun shone, the paler and sadder Snegurochka grew.

One beautiful spring morning Lel came to Snegurochka's little window and pleaded with her to come out with him, just once, for just a moment. For a long while Snegurochka refused to listen, but finally her heart could no longer resist Lel's pleas, and she went with her beloved to the edge of the village.

"Lel, oh my Lel, play your flute for me alone!" she asked. She stood before Lel, barely alive, her feet tingling, not a drop of blood in her pale face!

Lel took out his flute and began to play Snegurochka's favorite air.

She listened to the song, and tears rolled down from her eyes. Then her feet melted beneath her; she fell onto the damp earth and suddenly vanished.

Lel saw nothing but a light mist rising from where she had fallen. The vapor rose, rose, and disappeared slowly in the blue sky. . . .

Lel took out his flute and began to play Snegurochka's favorite air.

VASSILISSA THE FAIR

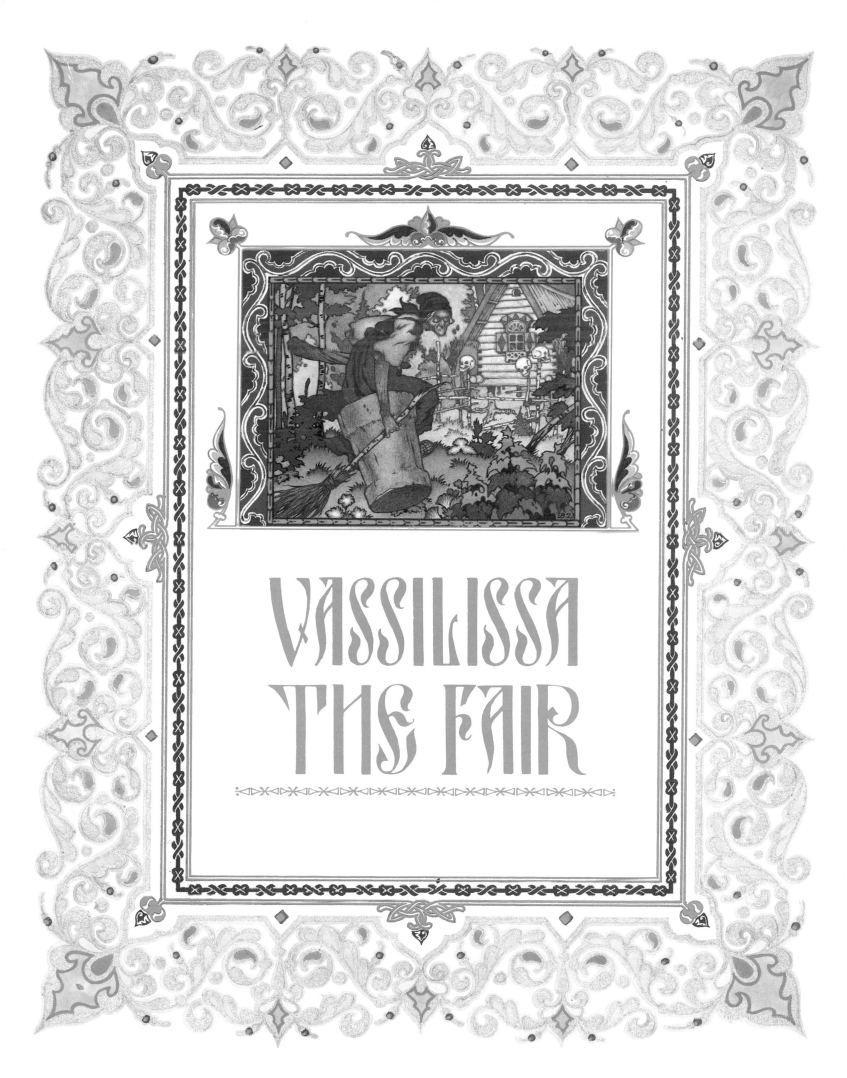

VASSILISSA THE FAIR

nce upon a time in a certain kingdom, there lived a merchant. He had been married for twelve years and had but one daughter, Vassilissa the Fair.

When the child was eight years old, her mother died. She summoned her daughter to her deathbed, took a doll from beneath the covers, gave it to her, and said:

"Listen, Vassilissochka! Remember my words and do what I say. I am dying. I leave you with my motherly blessing and this doll; keep it close always, and show it to no one. If misfortune befalls you, give the doll something to eat and ask its advice. She will eat, then tell you what to do."

The mother embraced her daughter and died.

After his wife's death, the merchant mourned as was proper, then thought of taking a second wife. He was a handsome man with many admirers, but a certain widow pleased him most. She was no longer young, had two daughters near Vassilissa's age, and was a good housekeeper and a good mother.

The merchant married her, but she was not a good mother to Vassilissa.

Vassilissa was the beauty of the village. The stepmother and her daughters were jealous of her beauty and burdened her with all the chores, hoping that she would grow thin and tired, burned by the wind and sun. The child led a hard life.

Yet Vassilissa never complained, and grew plumper and more beautiful, while the stepmother and her daughters grew thinner and uglier, though they did nothing but sit around all day with their arms folded, just like fine ladies.

How did she manage? It was the doll who helped Vassilissa. Without her, she could never have finished her work. Vassilissa often ate nothing herself, and saved her food for her doll. At night, when everyone was in bed, she would lock herself in her little room and talk to the doll: ❖•❖•❖

"Here little doll, eat this and listen to my woes! I live in my father's house, but I never have fun; my wicked stepmother tortures me. Tell me what to do, how to bear this life!"

The doll ate, gave her good advice, comforted her, and, in the morning, finished all her work for her. Vassilissa was told to rest in the shade and pick flowers; the flower beds were weeded, the cabbages watered, the water jars filled and the cooking fire started. The doll also showed Vassilissa a little herb to prevent sunburn. It was good to live with the little doll.

Several years passed; Vassilissa grew up and was ready for marriage. All the village youths came to ask for her hand; none of them looked at her stepsisters. The stepmother grew more disagreeable than ever and told the suitors:

"We will not give our youngest daughter before her two older sisters!" And, having sent them away, she got even with Vassilissa by beating her.

One day, the merchant had to leave on business for a long time. The stepmother went to live in another house; near this house was a dense forest; in the forest was a clearing; in the clearing there was a hut; and in this hut lived Baba Yaga. She let no one near her and devoured men as if they were chickens.

Once installed in her new house, the stepmother sent Vassilissa into the forest on every pretext, but Vassilissa always came safely back. The doll showed her the way to avoid Baba Yaga's hut.

Autumn came. One evening the stepmother gave the three girls their nightly tasks. She told one to make lace, one to knit stockings, and she told Vassilissa to spin. The mother put out the fire and left one candle burning for the girls to work by, then went to bed.

The candle burned low. One of the stepsisters took the snuffers to cut down the wick, but she extinguished the candle as if by accident, as her mother had told her to do.

"What shall we do now?" cried the sisters. "There is no fire in all the house and we have not finished our tasks. We must get some from Baba Yaga!"

"I can see by the pins," said the one who was making lace, "I will not go."

"Neither will I," said the one who was knitting a stocking. "I can see by the needles."

"You go and get some fire," they both cried. "You go to Baba Yaga," and they pushed Vassilissa out of the room.

Vassilissa went to her chamber, gave her doll supper, and said, "Eat, little doll, and listen to my woe! They are sending me to Baba Yaga for fire, and Baba Yaga will eat me up!"

The doll ate and its eyes shone like two candles. "Fear nothing, Vassilissochka! Go where they say, only take me along. When I am with you, Baba Yaga can do you no harm!"

Vassilissa made ready, put the doll in her pocket, made the sign of the cross, and walked trembling into the deep forest.

Suddenly a knight on horseback galloped past her. He was pale, dressed in white; his horse was white and its harness was white. Dawn began to break.

She went farther, and another knight galloped past her. He was red, dressed in red, and his horse was red. The sun began to climb.

Vassilissa went on, through the day, through the night and the next day. Toward evening she came to a clearing where Baba Yaga's hut stood. The fence around the hut was made of human bones. On the bones were stuck human skulls with glaring eyes. In place of a lock there was a jawbone with sharp teeth.

Vassilissa was paralyzed with fear and stood quite still. Suddenly another knight appeared. He was black, dressed in black, on a black horse. He galloped up to Baba Yaga's door and vanished, and night fell.

But the darkness did not last long, for all the eyes in the skulls on the fence gleamed, and the clearing was lit as if by daylight. Vassilissa trembled with fear, but, not knowing where to flee, held her ground.

Soon she heard a terrible noise in the forest; tree boughs creaked and dry leaves crackled. Baba Yaga drove out of the forest in a mortar, steering it with a pestle, sweeping away her tracks with a broom. She went to the door, stopped, sniffed the air, and cried:

"Aha! I smell a red-haired girl. Who goes there?"

Vassilissa, shivering with dread, went up to her, curtsied low, and said:

"It is I, Grandmother! My stepsisters have sent me to ask you for fire!"

"Yes," said Baba Yaga, "I know them. Stay with me, work for me a while, and I will give you fire. If you do not, I will eat you up!"

She went to the door and shouted:

"Ho! My strong bolts, draw back! My strong lock, spring open!" The door opened and Baba Yaga went in, whistling and whirling. Vassilissa followed and the door slammed shut.

Inside, Baba Yaga stretched out and said to Vassilissa: "Bring me whatever is in the oven. I want to eat!" Vassilissa lit a stick from the skulls on the fence, poked food from the oven, and brought it to Baba Yaga; she brought food enough for ten men. From the cellar she brought kvass, and mead and wine. The old hag ate and drank everything up. Nothing was left for Vassilissa but a little cabbage soup, a crust of bread, and a piece of suckling pig.

Baba Yaga lay down to sleep and said:

"Tomorrow, when I leave, make sure to sweep the house, make the dinner and do the wash, go to the bin, get a quart of oats, and sift out every speck of dust. Do all that or I will eat you up!"

When she had given these orders she began to snore. Vassilissa put the leftovers in front of the doll, burst into tears and said:

"Eat, little doll, and listen to my woe! Baba Yaga has given me so much work. She threatens to eat me up if I cannot finish. Help me!"

The doll answered:

"Fear not, Fair Vassilissa! Eat, pray, and go to sleep. Night will bring help."

When Vassilissa awoke the next morning, Baba Yaga was already up, looking out the window. The eyes in the skulls had dimmed. The white horseman raced by; dawn came. Baba Yaga whirled into the courtyard and whistled; her mortar and pestle and broom appeared. The red horseman raced by; the sun rose.

Baba Yaga climbed into the mortar, thrust with the pestle, and left, brushing her tracks away with the broom.

Vassilissa, left alone, gazed around and wondered where to begin. But the work was already done; the doll had sifted out the last grains of oats.

"Oh, my savior," said Vassilissa to the doll. "You have delivered me from harm!"

"You have only dinner left to prepare," answered the doll as she climbed back into Vassilissa's pocket. "Be quick, for God's sake, then rest for your health!"

That evening Vassilissa set the table and waited for Baba Yaga; twilight fell, the black horseman galloped by, and it was night. Only the lights in the skulls' eyes glowed.

The trees creaked, dry leaves crackled; Baba Yaga arrived. Vassilissa met her.

"Is everything done?"

"Yes, Grandmother, please look," said Vassilissa.

Baba Yaga looked around and was furious not to find anything wrong.

"Good!" Then she called: "Faithful servants, devoted friends, take my oats!"

Three pairs of dwarfs appeared; they seized the oats and bore them out of sight.

Baba Yaga ate supper, got ready for bed, and once more gave orders to Vassilissa: ❖❖❖

"Tomorrow you will do the same as today. In addition, take a poppy from the chest and clean every grain of dust from it. Someone, out of spite, has dirtied my poppy!" She turned to the wall and started to snore.

She went farther, and another knight galloped past her.

Vassilissa fed her doll, who told her as before:

"Pray to God and go to sleep. The night will bring help. All will be done!"

In the morning Baba Yaga once more left in the mortar, and Vassilissa and the doll did the chores. The old woman returned, looked all about, and shouted:

"Faithful servants, devoted friends, make me some poppy-seed oil!" Three pairs of dwarfs appeared, and took the poppy away.

Baba Yaga sat down to dinner; she ate while Vassilissa stood by in silence.

"Why do you not speak?" said Baba Yaga. "You stand there like a dumbbell!"

"I did not dare," answered Vassilissa, "but with your permission, could I ask you a question?"

"Ask, but beware! Too many questions will make you grow old!"

"I would like to ask you, Grandmother, about something I saw. As I came here I passed a white knight, dressed in white, on a white horse. Who is he?"

"He is Day," answered Baba Yaga.

"Then I passed a red knight dressed in red, on a red horse. Who is he?"

"He is the Red Sun," answered Baba Yaga.

"And who is the black knight who passed near the door, Grandmother?"

"He is my Dark Night. They are my faithful servants."

Vassilissa remembered the three pairs of dwarfs and said nothing.

"Why not ask more?" said Baba Yaga.

"I have asked enough, for, as you say, too many questions make one grow old."

"It is well that you asked only about things outside the house. I eat up people who are too nosy. Now tell me this: How did you manage to do all the work?"

"With my mother's blessing."

"So that's it! Then get away as fast as you can! No one blessed may stay with me." She dragged Vassilissa from the room and threw her out the door, took a skull with burning eyes from the fence, stuck it on a spike, and gave it to her, saying: "Here is fire for your stepmother's daughters. Take it! Was it not for that they sent you here?"

Vassilissa ran home, by the light of the skull, which went out with the dawn. By evening of the next day she reached the house, and was going to throw the skull away.

"Surely," she thought, "they no longer need fire." But just then she heard a voice from the skull: "Do not throw me away. Bring me to your stepmother."

She looked at her stepmother's house, and, seeing no light at the windows, decided to go there with the skull. For once she was welcomed and told that since she left they had been without fire. They had been unable to make any, and the fire they had borrowed from their neighbors had gone out as soon as they brought it into the room.

"Perhaps your fire will burn!" said the stepmother. They brought in the skull, and when it glared at the stepmother and her daughters it burned them. They tried to hide, but no matter where they went, the eyes followed them; by morning they were burned to ashes in a corner. Only Vassilissa remained untouched.

In the morning Vassilissa buried the skull, locked the house, went into town, and lodged with an old woman who had no family. She lived with her, awaiting her father's return. One day she said to the old woman:

"Grandmother, I feel idle with no work to do. Go and buy me some fine flax. I would like to spin!"

The old woman bought some fine flax, and Vassilissa began to spin. She worked hard, and the skein became thin as a hair. She made much yarn, but when it was ready to weave, no combs could be found fine enough, and no one would weave it.

Vassilissa turned to her doll, who said: ❖◆❖◆

"Bring me any old comb, any old spindle, and some horse hair. I will do it for you."

Vassilissa brought everything, then went to bed, and during the night the doll wove fine linen.

By winter's end all the linen had been woven, and it was so fine that it could be drawn through the eye of a needle. In the spring, they bleached it and Vassilissa said to the old woman: ❖◆❖◆

"Go sell this linen, Grandmother, and keep the money for yourself!"

The old woman looked at it and exclaimed: ❖◆❖◆

"Oh, my child! No one but the Tsar could wear such fine cloth! I will take it to court!"

The old woman went to the Tsar's palace and walked back and forth in front of a window. The Tsar saw her and said: ❖◆❖◆

"Old woman, what do you want?"

"Your Royal Majesty, I have here some marvelous cloth. I will show it to no one but you!"

The Tsar ordered the old woman brought in, and when he saw the cloth, was amazed.

"What do you want for it?" he asked.

"It is beyond price, Little Father. I have brought it to you as a present."

The Tsar thanked the old woman and sent her back home laden with gifts.

Vassilissa went before the Tsar.

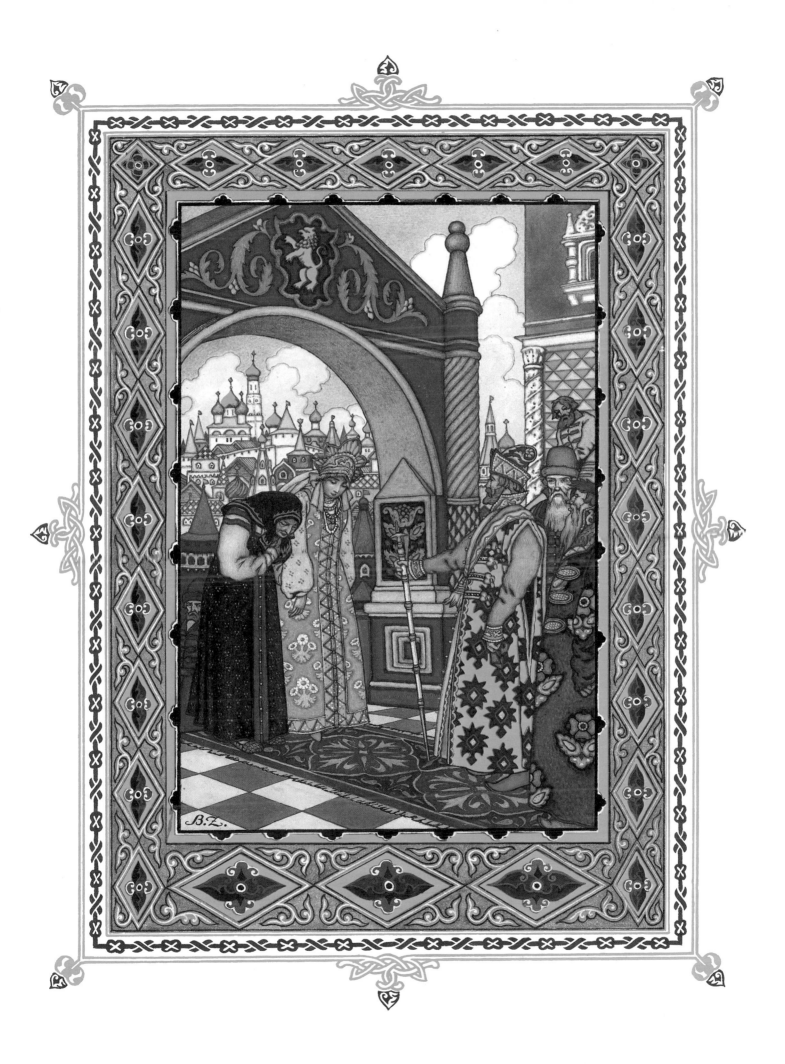

The Tsar wanted shirts made from the linen, but no seamstress could be found who could make them. At last he sent for the old woman and said:

"You were able to spin and to weave this fine cloth. Could you also make it into shirts?"

"It was not I who wove and spun the linen," said the old woman, "but my adopted daughter."

"If that is so, let her also sew it into shirts!"

The old woman returned home and told all to Vassilissa.

"I knew that I should have to do this task!"

She shut herself in her room, set to work, and sewed without cease, until she had made a dozen shirts.

The old woman brought the shirts to the Tsar, while Vassilissa bathed, combed her hair, dressed, then sat by the window and waited. She saw the Tsar's envoy come toward the house; he entered the room and said:

"The Tsar wishes to see the artist who sewed him shirts, to reward her with his royal hands!"

Vassilissa went before the Tsar. The moment he saw her he fell deeply in love.

"I will never part from you, fair maid!" he said. "You must be my wife!"

So the Tsar took Vassilissa with his white hands, made her sit beside him, and then and there celebrated the marriage. Vassilissa's father returned; he rejoiced at his daughter's good fortune and stayed on at court.

Vassilissa brought the old woman to live with her, and, until the end of her days, kept her doll always in her pocket.

The illustrations in this book are reproduced in five colors
from the original gouache paintings. The calligraphy is a modified version
of the original hand lettering. Text has been set in Linotype Caslon and
was composed by American Book–Stratford Press, Inc., Brattleboro, Vermont.
The book is printed on Warren's Lustro Offset Enamel Dull. Color separations
were made by Capper, Inc., Knoxville, Tennessee. The book was printed
by Rae Publishing Company, Inc., Cedar Grove, New Jersey, and bound by
American Book–Stratford Press, Inc., Saddle Brook, New Jersey.